The Little Shot Series

The Little Shot

By Tasha Eizinger

Illustrated by Lauren Moyer

GROUND TRUTH PRESS

NASHUA, NEW HAMPSHIRE

To my sweet Little Shot and ALL the Little Shots

Publisher's Cataloging-In-Publication Data
(Prepared by The Donohue Group, Inc.)

Names: Eizinger, Tasha. | Moyer, Lauren,
    illustrator.
Title: The Little Shot / by Tasha Eizinger ;
    illustrated by Lauren Moyer.
Description: Nashua, New Hampshire : Ground
    Truth Press, [2018] | Series: The Little
    Shot series | Interest age level: 003-008.
    | Summary: "What if you had such a big
    goal that you had no clue how to
    accomplish it? Little Shot is simply a
    star with the dream of becoming a shooting
    star. Follow the ups and downs of her
    journey. She isn't sure if she can become
    a Big Shot, but she knows she has to give
    it a solid effort!"--Provided by
    publisher.
Identifiers: ISBN 978-0-9908303-5-1 (trade
    paperback) | ISBN 0-9908303-5-7 (trade
    paperback)
Subjects: LCSH: Stars--Juvenile fiction. |
    Meteors--Juvenile fiction. | Goal
    (Psychology)--Juvenile fiction. | CYAC:
    Stars--Fiction. | Meteors--Fiction. | Goal
    (Psychology)--Fiction.
Classification: LCC PZ7.1.E59 Li 2018 | DDC
    [E]--dc23

2017942649

The Little Shot

The Little Shot series

Published by
GROUND TRUTH PRESS
P. O. Box 7313
Nashua, NH 03060-7313
For more information about our books, kindly visit our website at *www.groundtruthpress.com.*

Editor: Bonnie Lyn Smith

First printing, 2018

Printed in the United States of America

Trade paperback ISBN-13: 978-0-9908303-5-1
Trade paperback ISBN-10: 0990830357

Dear Parents and Educators:

Children rise to the bar we set for them. Yes, it takes patience, time, and consistency to allow them the opportunity to learn. Isn't that how we learn as well? As I wrote this story, I had friends and family read it. I wanted their feedback. You may also agree with some of them that the vocabulary and content are too challenging in this book.

My daughter is 19 months old (at this time), and I use more adultlike vocabulary with her. It's rather interesting that she not only understands most of what I am saying, but she also has a solid vocabulary for her age. When I taught fifth grade, my students were a bit frustrated at the beginning of the year because they were unfamiliar with many of the words I was using. However, by the end of the year, their reading comprehension, writing skills, and understanding increased significantly. Why not take some time to complete the activities at the end of this story to guide them as they learn an enriched vocabulary and valuable life lessons? Raise the bar for your child(ren), and see how far they can go!

My hope is that this book adds value to your life and to your child's life. Dream big, and always remember to wish upon a shooting star!

Blessings,
Tasha Eizinger

Little Shot really thought about this.

This doesn't sound very exciting. It sounds like a lot of work!

Her dad chuckled and said, "Of course it's a lot of work. That's why there aren't very many Big Shots. You have to be willing to pay the price. But, sweet girl, don't you think those Big Shots have a lot of fun?"

Little Shot's grandma was so wise and taught her the importance of adding value and uplifting others by asking herself every morning, "Who can I make smile today?" Since her grandma was much older than Little Shot, she had a different perspective on life.

Little Shot said,

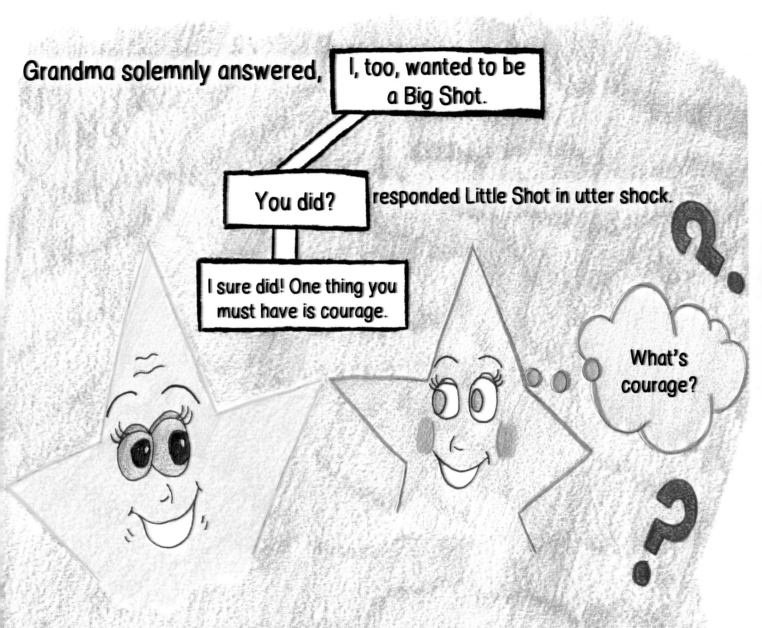

Grandma solemnly answered, "I, too, wanted to be a Big Shot.

You did? responded Little Shot in utter shock.

I sure did! One thing you must have is courage.

What's courage?

"Courage is leading from your heart in spite of your fear and despite the stars who will want to drag you down."

Her grandma continued, "I want you to keep asking these types of questions as you become a Big Shot. That way your dream can become a reality. Looking back on my long life, sweetheart, I realize that it's not the chances I took and failed that have caused me the most pain. It's the pain of regret of the chances I didn't take. Now, it's a little too late for me to become a Big Shot, but I'm here to support you every step of the way. I have different goals and dreams now than I did when I was your age. However, I'm still learning, growing, and becoming the best star that I can be."

Little Shot gave her grandma a big hug and a kiss on the cheek and went along her way.

Here's my becoming a Big Shot list...

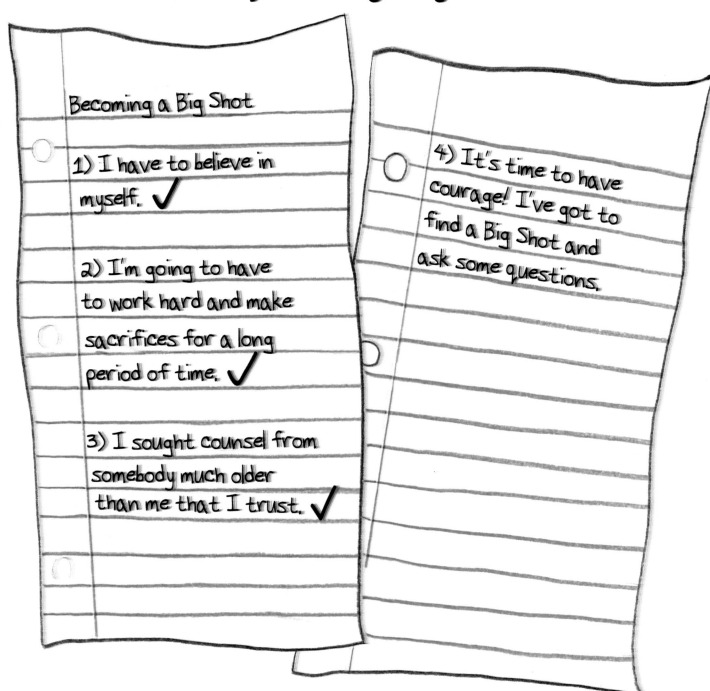

Little Shot felt her heart race, her palms sweat, and she felt shaky.

Maybe, I don't really want to be a Big Shot. Maybe, I'll be okay with just being an ordinary star hanging in the sky. People like those, you know! They do enjoy looking at them, and they are very beautiful. Eventually, when their purpose has been fulfilled they fade.

Deep down inside Little Shot knew her calling and purpose in this world was to be a Big Shot. Slowly, she started walking toward the Big Shots.

On her way, she found some of her classmates who were also thinking about what they wanted to be when they grew up. Some of them were fine with being ordinary stars in the sky. Some of them wanted to be a part of a constellation and were planning a way to make a new one. Some of them wanted to be a comet for the fame and fortune, but they weren't willing to work for it.

I want to be a part of a constellation.

I want to be a comet.

Little Shot was the only one that wanted to be a shooting star. Some of them laughed at her, and others made fun of her.

She walked away feeling dejected. Some of her friends said,

I guess you can give it a try. If it doesn't work out, you can join us in the sky.

She still felt defeated hearing the doubt in their words. They obviously didn't believe in her even though they appeared supportive.

One friend said,

I've known you for a long time. You are smart and hardworking. Just learn the steps, and I believe you can make it happen.

Little Shot was so grateful for this dear friend and promised herself when she learned how to become a Big Shot, she would help her friend who believed in her from the beginning.

Clinging to the words of her mom, dad, grandma, and friend, she mustered up the courage to speak with the Big Shots.

The Big Shots were warming up for yet another night of fun and another night of inspiration and hope.

She walked up to one of them and bashfully asked,

The Big Shot smiled at her, beaming with pride in the Little Shot's courage and said,

Little Shot was rather surprised and very thankful for the Big Shot's generous offer.

She started learning and discovered it was very hard work. She could understand why other stars didn't want to do this. The little mustard seed of faith in her dream had been planted deep in her heart. She knew if she persevered with a determined spirit that she could keep going and make it happen. Many years down the road with lots of practice and taking one step at a time, she had her big night. She prayed like she had never prayed before.

1...2...3...

Oh no! It's not working! What's happening?

shouted Little Shot in desperation. Little Shot was falling down, not shooting across the sky!

Luckily, she felt a hand reach down to carry her. When the Big Shots and Little Shot returned to their starting point in the sky, Little Shot was so embarrassed. She had failed! It didn't work! What had she done wrong? All of her time and energy was wasted.

Big Shot could see the distraught look and anguish on Little Shot's face and remembered how it felt on his first attempt.

Little Shot was amazed at the Big Shot's response and paused for quite awhile thinking of an answer, "I'm really glad that I did it in spite of my fear. I also had a really strong start."

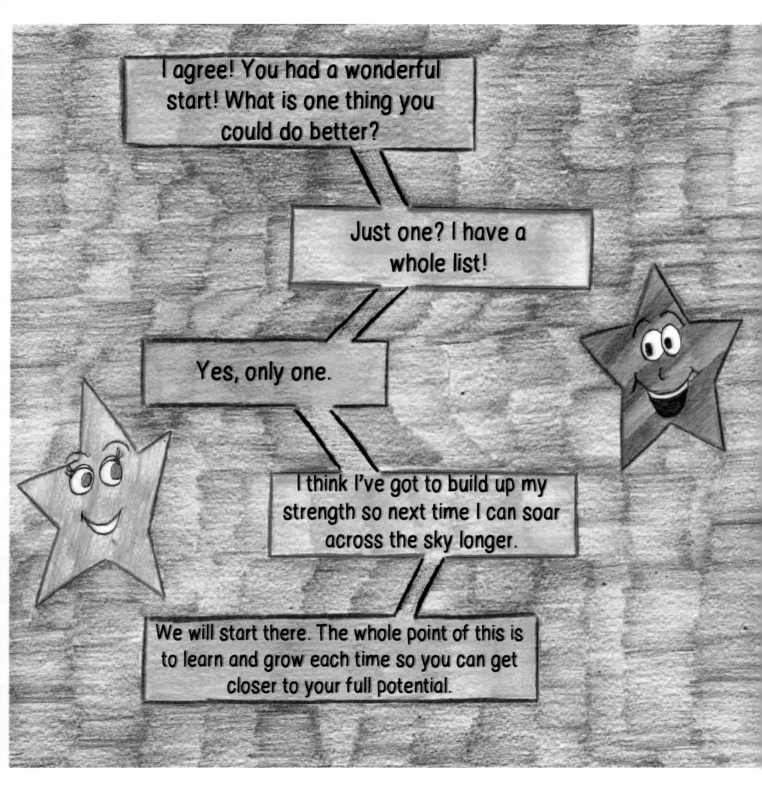

Little Shot went back to work. Some nights she did a little better, and some nights she did a little worse. She felt like she would take three steps forward and two or four steps backward.

The fire in her heart kept her going.

Finally, Little Shot could tell she was truly ready. She felt different on this particular night. There was a sense of knowing that she had grown through this journey...enough to really soar!

Activities for Parents and Educators

The following are suggested activities for how to engage with your children (or students) after reading this book:

1) Look up synonyms for new words your child doesn't know yet.

2) Discuss: What is a wish you once had, and what did you learn along the way? What is your child's big goal this year? Who are some people who could mentor your child, and what is a basic action plan to make it happen?

3) Look up pictures of constellations, shooting stars, and comets. What makes each one similar to and different from each other?

4) Approach a grandparent or go to a local nursing home to interview someone there. What have been some of his or her most meaningful life lessons? If this person could go back and do something different, what would it be? If he or she could do something the same way, what would it be? Which book was most impactful in this person's life? Why?

5) Choose a favorite quote from the book. Write it out, decorate it, laminate it, and frame it. Hang it in your child's room.

6) Write a letter to your child explaining why you believe in him or her. What special qualities does your child possess that can plant seeds of belief in him or her?

7) Discuss each lesson Little Shot learned:
   a) Dream big.
   b) Believe in yourself.
   c) Work hard.
   d) Make sacrifices.
   e) Seek counsel from an older person who can be trusted.
   f) Have courage.
   g) Seek mentorship from someone successful in the area where you want to succeed.

8) Discuss doubts that you have experienced on your journey toward your goals and doubts your child may have as well. What are some ways to create belief and action in spite of those fears?

9) Write a letter to a friend or family member who inspires and encourages your child.

10) One of the best ways to learn and improve is by making mistakes. Ask your child every evening: What is something you did today to mess up? What did you learn?

11) How do you think Little Shot felt after becoming a Big Shot? Write a poem about Little Shot's journey.

12) Keep an eye out in the evenings for shooting stars, and remember to make a wish!